illustrated by
Simone Shin

THANK YOU, GARDEN

Beach Lane Books • New York London Toronto Sydney New Delhi

Garden ready,

Garden so much

work to do!

Garden rock
and garden water

Garden son
and garden daughter

Garden dig and garden play

Garden filling up the day

Garden bed

and garden plot

Garden proper,

garden not

Garden hardly makes a sound

growing, slowly, underground

Sometimes rainy,

sometimes dry

Garden soaking up the sky

Garden path meets garden gate

Garden wait . . .

and wait . . .

and wait

Garden frog

and worm and bees

Garden berries,

beets, and peas

Garden growing like a child.

rosy,

leggy,

fresh, and wild—

Wild in this muddy mess,

garden, thank you. . . .

Garden, yes!

For Kathi, Susan, Anne, and Lindsey,
who help me grow—L. G. S.

To Dylan and Ryan—S. S.

BEACH LANE BOOKS
An imprint of Simon & Schuster Children's Publishing Division
1230 Avenue of the Americas, New York, New York 10020
Text copyright © 2020 by Elizabeth Garton Scanlon
Illustrations copyright © 2020 by Simone Shin
All rights reserved, including the right of reproduction in whole or in part in any form.
BEACH LANE BOOKS is a trademark of Simon & Schuster, Inc.
For information about special discounts for bulk purchases, please contact Simon & Schuster Special Sales
at 1-866-506-1949 or business@simonandschuster.com.
The Simon & Schuster Speakers Bureau can bring authors to your live event.
For more information or to book an event, contact the Simon & Schuster Speakers Bureau
at 1-866-248-3049 or visit our website at www.simonspeakers.com.
Book design by Lauren Rille
The text for this book was set in Artlessness.
The illustrations for this book were rendered in acrylic paint, watercolor, and Photoshop.
Manufactured in China
1219 SCP
First Edition
10 9 8 7 6 5 4 3 2 1
Library of Congress Cataloging-in-Publication Data
Names: Scanlon, Elizabeth Garton, author. | Shin, Simone, illustrator.
Title: Thank you, garden / Liz Garton Scanlon ; illustrated by Simone Shin.
Description: First edition. | New York : Beach Lane Books, [2020] |
Summary: Illustrations and rhyming text explore a community garden
and what grows there, from flowers and fruit to friendships.
Identifiers: LCCN 2019010138 | ISBN 9781481403504 (hardcover : alk. paper) |
ISBN 9781481403511 (eBook)
Subjects: | CYAC: Stories in rhyme. | Community gardens–Fiction. | Gardening–Fiction.
Classification: LCC PZ8.3.S2798 Tf 2020 | DDC [E]–dc23 LC record available at
https://lccn.loc.gov/2019010138